Dedicated to the memory of Shane Bownes.
And to all those giving me courage on my journey with cancer ~ C H W

To all of my siblings: Agneta, Gisela, Anna, Sara, Hampus,
Emma and Fredrik. So lucky to have you all ~ Å G

LITTLE TIGER PRESS LTD,
an imprint of the Little Tiger Group
1 Coda Studios, 189 Munster Road, London SW6 6AW
www.littletiger.co.uk
First published in Great Britain 2020
Text copyright © Clare Helen Welsh 2020
Illustrations copyright © Åsa Gilland 2020

Clare Helen Welsh and Åsa Gilland have asserted
their rights to be identified as the author and illustrator of this
work under the Copyright, Designs and Patents Act, 1988

A CIP catalogue record for this book is available from the British Library
All rights reserved • ISBN 978-1-78881-578-9
Printed in China • LTP/1800/2933/0120
10 9 8 7 6 5 4 3 2 1

FSC
www.fsc.org
MIX
Paper from
responsible sources
FSC® C020056

the *perfect* SHELTER

Clare Helen Welsh

Åsa Gilland

LITTLE TIGER

LONDON

At first nobody knew.
It was the perfect day,
it was the perfect weather . . .

. . . to build a shelter in the woods.
I called to my sister,
"Fetch some sticks."
She called to me,
"Stack them high."

We sang as we worked and
we worked as we sang.

"It's the perfect, perfect shelter!"

But then something changed. She looked the same. Except she wasn't quite. Mum and Dad didn't want me to worry.

"Your sister's just a bit tired," they said.

That night a wild wind blew.

HOOOOOWOOOOO!

OUR DEN

But the wind was no match for us!

I called to my sister,
"Fetch more sticks."
She called to me,
"Stack them higher."

We sang as we worked
and we worked as we sang.

"It's the perfect, perfect shelter!"

But something still wasn't right.
And I knew it was bad because
people were crying.

Then they told me
my sister was sick.

That night a river of rain
fell from the sky.

RUSH, RUSH, ROAR!

Of course, a little bit of water couldn't hurt us. Our shelter just needed some mending, some fixing . . .

Only when I called to my sister to, "Find some leaves,"
she was with the doctors.

And when I called to her to, "Cover the cracks,"
she was having an operation.

I didn't sing.
I couldn't work.
I was too worried.

In the hospital I felt cross, and sad,
and frightened, all at the same time.
"How did it get there?"
"Why can't she come home?"
"Why MY sister?"
I tried my best to listen . . .

But I saw a bright light.

FLASH!

I heard a loud sound.

CRACK!

And when we got home,
our perfect shelter
was no more.
   But I didn't even care.
I just wanted my sister
to be better.

Days turned to nights.

Nights turned to days.

The storm eased.

Snow settled.

My sister was **stronger** and **brighter**.
So I told her about the shelter.
I told her about the snow.

Then she whispered,
"I think it's the perfect time,
I think it's the perfect place,
to build a shelter . . ."

"...right here, right now!"
I wasn't sure at first.

But then she got up and told me to, "Fetch some sheets."

So I called to her, "Find a broom."

We sang as we worked and we worked as we sang.

"It's the perfect, perfect shelter!"

And all the time, neither of us
noticed . . .

...we were smiling.

Now we make plans to go back to the woods to ride out the toughest storms. But until then . . .

... today's the perfect day
to build a shelter
and **be together.**